Mrs Tickler's CARAVAN

MRS. TICKLER'S CARAVAN

A STORY FOR CHILDREN

WRITTEN AND ILLUSTRATED BY

CECIL ALDIN

NEW YORK
CHARLES SCRIBNER'S SONS
1931

CONTENTS

MRS. TICKLER'S CARAVAN

MRS TICKLERS CARAVAN

BY CECIL ALDIN

TO INTRODUCE THE MAGIC HANDKERCHIEF

ATISH-SHOO! Atish-shoo!! Atish-shoo!!! sneezed Mr. Tickler. Mr. Tickler was always sneezing.

"For goodness' sake go to the fair and buy yourself a large handkerchief," said Mrs. Tickler as she came down the steps of her caravan, opening her umbrella.

A-tish-shoo! A-tish-shoo!!!! once more, sneezed Mr. Tickler for the twentieth time that morning.

But it was because poor Mr. Tickler had nothing to blow his nose with that he could never stop sneezing.

Mr. Tickler goes to the Fair.

Mr. Tickler led a hard life. He lived in a little covered cart drawn by Dumpy the Donkey, but he was never allowed inside Mrs. Tickler's beautiful caravan, because he snored all night and sneezed all day.

" Go to the fair," said Mrs. Tickler once again, " and get a large one, big enough to blow your sneeze away—you'll never get rid of sneezes until you give your nose a good blow," at the same time, to Mr. Tickler's astonishment, producing a bright brand-new half-crown piece.

Now Mr. Tickler had never had so much money given to him before by Mrs. Tickler, and he was terrified that she might change her mind before he could start for the fair to make his purchase, so he ran across to his little cart as quickly as he could in order to change into his best clothes, which consisted of a bowler hat rather too small for him and his coat with the big pockets. Soon afterwards he was hastening away towards the fair, holding the new half-crown tightly in his hand.

When he arrived at the fair ground there were so many things for him to see—swings, round-a-bouts, cocoa-nut shies, cheap-jacks and other things

Mr. Tickler buys the Magic Handkerchief.

—that it was some time before he found what he wanted.

At last he stood open-mouthed watching a cheap-jack sell clocks guaranteed to go for ever, medicines that were certain to cure you of any disease under the sun, and umbrellas that would keep out the heaviest rainfall. Then, just as the last watch had been sold and the crowd were beginning to disperse, the auctioneer produced an enormous red spotted handkerchief from a cardboard box, and Mr. Tickler at once began to shake all over with excitement. He was, however, a careful man, so before making an offer for the handkerchief he asked the cheap-jack in his high-pitched voice, whether the handkerchief was guaranteed to cure sneezing.

"Sneezing?" shouted the seller; "sneezing? why, I'll guarantee this handkerchief to cure all boils, blisters, or bunions, and drive away all diseases of the heart, liver or stomach. I'll make a gift of this wonderful handkerchief to you, sir, for five shillings."

Mr. Tickler, as we know, had only half-a-crown, but he wanted more than ever to possess that enormous handkerchief.

"Half-a-crown is all I've got," he murmured nervously, feeling everyone in the crowd was looking at him.

"Half-a-dollar," shouted the cheap-jack in his face; "why, you couldn't buy the box it's in for that," and after a pause to see if anyone would bid more, he continued, "but I like your face, sir, and I'll make you a present of the handkerchief for half-a-dollar."

Mr. Tickler handed over his half-crown, and the cheap-jack passed him his purchase, and that was how the magic handkerchief came into Mr. Tickler's possession.

When Mr. Tickler got home to his little cart that night it was very late, and he was so sleepy that he could hardly get into his red flannel nightshirt and woolly bed-socks before dropping off to sleep, but he did *not* forget to put up his blue umbrella to keep the drops off his feet in case it rained. Mr. Tickler slept that night without snoring, peacefully dreaming of the wonders of his magic handkerchief.

He could hardly get into his nightshirt.

MR. TICKLER
TRIES THE MAGIC HANDKERCHIEF
FOR THE FIRST TIME

MR. TICKLER
TRIES THE MAGIC HANDKERCHIEF FOR THE FIRST TIME

THE sun was fast coming up above the tree-tops when Mr. Tickler was awakened by Dumpy the donkey pulling off one of his precious bed-socks, and Nancy's foal playfully pulling his hair; but the first thing he did, even before he shooed them away, was to feel for his handkerchief, and at that moment his usual morning sneezing fit started.

"You can't stop the sneezes without blowing your nose," quoted Mr. Tickler, so, grasping his nose firmly with the handkerchief, he gave a mighty blow. The effect was astonishing. Dumpy was blown over yards away, and the foal had the shock of his life.

"This is grand," said Mr. Tickler as he crawled out of bed. "I must try it again."

The Effect was

Extraordinary !

MR. TICKLER
TRIES HIS MAGIC HANDKERCHIEF FOR
THE SECOND TIME

AT that moment he caught sight of Mr. Cock-a-doodle-do and Mrs. Cock-a-doodle-don't a few yards away scratching about for their breakfast. Not stopping to put on his clothes, he jumped out of the donkey-cart, just as he was in his red flannel night-shirt and began a series of nose-blowings in the direct aim for the Cock-a-doodle-dos.

At every successive blow they were shot yards in the air, much to Mr. Tickler's amusement, and he fairly rocked with laughter, finally blowing them back on to the top of the cart in his excitement.

"There is no knowing what I can do with this handkerchief," said Mr. Tickler.

But he there and then decided

not to tell Mrs. Tickler about it.

MR. TICKLER
TRIES HIS HANDKERCHIEF FOR
THE THIRD TIME

MR. TICKLER
TRIES HIS HANDKERCHIEF FOR
THE THIRD TIME

As Mr. Tickler blew the astonished Cock-a-doodles on to the top of the cart, Mrs. Tickler's head in curling papers appeared from the door of her van. Mrs. Tickler did not look her best in the early morning.

" Where's my morning tea ? " shouted the lady.

Now in the excitement of chasing the chickens Mr. Tickler had quite forgotten to get his wife's tea, and now, try as he would, he could not get the fire to light. Once again he thought of his new purchase, and with only one nose-blow had a roaring fire burning and the kettle soon boiling.

" This handkerchief," said Mr. Tickler to himself as he carried Mrs. Tickler's tea to the van, " is going to be very useful."

27

" This handkerchief

is going to be very useful."

MR. TICKLER
TRIES HIS HANDKERCHIEF FOR
THE FOURTH TIME

MR. TICKLER
TRIES HIS HANDKERCHIEF FOR THE FOURTH TIME

ABOUT an hour afterwards, and when Mrs. Tickler had already started down the road in her caravan, Dumpy refused to start. Now sometimes Dumpy did this, and when she did she was very firm about it. No whacking with the blue umbrella made any impression upon her until she herself decided she would move forward. Mr. Tickler beat her and then tried coaxing her, but with no avail, until he again thought of his magic handkerchief.

This he knew would be a real test as to its magical qualities, for when once Dumpy had all four feet planted firmly on the ground, she took a great deal of moving.

One loud blow on Mr. Tickler's nose shot Dumpy forward and gave her a lesson she would not be likely to forget, and in a few moments the

" Marvellous ! "

said Mr. Tickler.

donkey-cart was peacefully trundling along behind Mrs. Tickler's caravan.

"Marvellous!" murmured Mr. Tickler, sitting on the shaft.

MR. TICKLER
TRIES HIS HANDKERCHIEF FOR
THE FIFTH TIME

MR. TICKLER
TRIES HIS HANDKERCHIEF FOR THE
FIFTH TIME

WHEN later on they came to a very steep hill and Nancy could not quite pull the heavy caravan to the top, Mr. Tickler walking behind, once again pulled out his red-spotted handkerchief.

Once more the result was extraordinary. Up to the top and over the brow of the hill went the caravan as if blown by the wind; but here was a dilemma Mr. Tickler had not foreseen, for Nancy now found the van impossible to stop, and Mr. Tickler saw his wife and her caravan dashing down the steepest hill he had ever seen towards the dangerous Char-a-banc corner where the char-a-bancs fall over every Wednesday.

Just for one moment Mr. Tickler wrung his hands in despair, but with great presence of mind saw a way out of the difficulty.

Seizing the spotted handkerchief by all four corners he took a run to the edge of the deep

coombe, on the other side of which Mrs. Tickler's
van was now rushing to destruction.

Jumping in the air as he reached the edge, the
great handkerchief opened out, making itself into a

parachute, and Mr. Tickler glided gracefully across the chasm, landing just in front of the caravan as it was about to reach Char-a-banc corner.

Once Mr. Tickler's feet touched the ground again, and almost before he had time to get his balance, the handkerchief was at his nose. One enormous blow aimed straight at Nancy's face stopped her as if by magic, and the whole cavalcade came to a standstill at the edge of the dangerous bend.

Mrs. Tickler had fainted in the van with fright, and with beads of perspiration on his brow Mr. Tickler hastened to bring her " to." It was a very near shave, and Mr. Tickler went hot and cold all over when he thought how it had been started.

" I must be more careful in using the power of the handkerchief," thought Mr. Tickler, but he did not even then tell Mrs. Tickler about it.

The handkerchief made itself into a parachute.

One enormous blow stopped Nancy.

41

MR. TICKLER
TRIES HIS HANDKERCHIEF FOR
THE SIXTH TIME

MR. TICKLER
TRIES HIS HANDKERCHIEF FOR THE SIXTH TIME

ONE day the Ticklers drove into a village and found a great commotion going on. On the village green a Circus tent was being fixed and all round were brightly-painted carts and horses and all sorts of strange people. Outside the Circus tent a man was sticking up bills showing a beautiful young lady on a snow-white horse, and a man with luxurious moustaches and a lot of gold medals, walking on a wire.

Now Mr. Tickler had never seen a Circus, and his eyes fairly started out of his head when he saw what was going on. I don't know whether Mrs. Tickler had ever seen one or not; at any rate she didn't seem very interested, but said crossly to her husband:

" Now then, what are you stopping for ? D'you

think they're going to give you a job looking after the lions?"

"Oo . . . oo," said Mr. Tickler, shivering at the thought. "Do you suppose they've got any lions?"

"How should I know?" snapped his wife. "I don't go round the world poking my nose into other people's business."

So Mr. Tickler drove on through the village, and nobody turned to look after them. Everybody was much too busy peering in the tents to see if they could see the Woman with Two Necks or the Genuine Pygmy from the Congo.

The Ticklers drove on to a common about half a mile down the road, where they camped and had their supper. Mrs. Tickler went into her van and was soon asleep, but Mr. Tickler was far too excited to sleep. He lay awake thinking of the young lady on the white horse and the man with the medals, and the lions, fierce and roaring. He *did* want to know if there were lions.

He wanted to know so much that when Mrs. Tickler had been asleep about half an hour, he got up and crept down the road towards the

village, in the hope that he might get to the green
before the village inn closed and hear a little news
about the Circus.

He got there just as the last of the stragglers were going off home.

"Good-night," they said pleasantly. "Bit late, aren't you?"

"I've just come to look round," explained Mr. Tickler, "and see what time the Circus starts."

For some reason or other the men seemed to find this terribly amusing.

"Ha! Ha! Ha!" they roared. "Wants to see what time the Circus starts." And they slapped one another on the back and held their sides with laughter. "He'll surely be in time," said one of them; "it don't start till three o'clock to-morrow. Ha! Ha! Ha!"

Mr. Tickler was rather hurt by their behaviour, but he wasn't going to be put off what he wanted to know.

"Have they got any lions in the Circus?" he asked when they paused for lack of breath.

"Oh, yes. They've got lions," said one of them, suddenly standing still. "And tigers too," he added solemnly.

"And hip . . . hip . . . hippipopotamuses," said another.

"And snakes," said a third. "You ought to see the snakes. Half-a-mile long and all deadly poison."

Mr. Tickler's eyes grew rounder and rounder.

"Goo," he said. "It must be a fine Circus."

But here the men burst out laughing again, so Mr. Tickler said "Good-night" rather stiffly and hurried back to the caravan, thankful to find that Mrs. Tickler had not woken up and missed him. But still he couldn't go to sleep for hours, thinking of the lions and the tigers and the snakes and the hippipopotamuses. He had never heard of them before. They must be something terrific. But how could he get to this wonderful Circus with no money and with Mrs. Tickler watching him all the time? He turned over plan after plan in his mind until at last he fell asleep.

In the morning he got up very early. He lit the fire briskly, took in Mrs. Tickler an extra strong cup of tea (she liked it very strong and sweet), fried the bacon to a turn, washed up and set to work to clean the van without being told once to do anything. Never had Mr. Tickler worked so hard before, and even Mrs. Tickler began to think that he must have some good points.

The Lions

Fierce and Roaring.

When the afternoon came and Mrs. Tickler, as usual, was going to retire to her van for her afternoon's nap, Mr. Tickler took his courage in both hands and said :

"Will you be wanting me for half an hour or so ? "

"Why ? " said the lady.

" I thought I'd just pop down into the village. There's one or two things we want there."

"What things ? " asked Mrs. Tickler sternly.

"B . . . b . . . butter, and m . . . m . . . matches and . . . "

"Well, here's a shilling," said Mrs. Tickler, " and don't forget the change. And don't be more than half an hour either," she added, turning round just before she went into her van.

Mr. Tickler could have hugged himself for joy. He scrambled into his coat and his bowler hat, carefully tucked his magic handkerchief in one of the big pockets, and flew down the road as fast as a hare. He had nearly got to the green when he remembered that although he had a shilling (one and threepence in fact, for he had three pennies of his own in his coat), he had to get some butter and some matches with it, as well as get into the Circus. And he also had to bring back some change.

The people came pouring into the Circus tent, flinging down sixpences and shillings, while Mr. Tickler was counting mournfully to himself, "There's half a pound of butter, that's eightpence, and three boxes of matches, that's threepence (I might get them for twopence), and sixpence to go in, but that makes one and fivepence and I've only got one and three, and if I didn't get the matches I'd still have to give her threepence change. Oh dear! If only somebody would drop a sixpence, or even a threepenny bit."

But nobody did. They all pushed heedlessly by Mr. Tickler who stood there looking at the man in charge of the pay box and turnstile: he was a fat man but he did not look at all sympathetic. Mr. Tickler felt it was no use asking him if he might have a seat at half price.

Mr. Tickler was so sorry for himself that the tears came into his eyes, and he put his hand in his pocket to get his handkerchief and wipe them away. Then the great idea came to him. He took out his magic handkerchief, unfolded it and

gave a loud blow, which sent the fat man flying out
of the pay box over the other side of the tent.

And while he was picking himself up, wondering where that awful gust of wind had come from, Mr. Tickler had nipped in under the canvas and taken his seat in the shilling part.

I expect you have seen a Circus, so you wouldn't be so thrilled by it all as Mr. Tickler was. He sat spellbound while little dogs bowed and shook hands and danced to the tune of " Pop goes the weasel." He gazed with his heart in his mouth on the man with the moustaches, walking in the air and balancing a pole. Suppose he fell, thought Mr. Tickler, how awful that would be. But he did not, and Mr. Tickler was both relieved and disappointed at the same time.

Then there was a banging of drums and in came the beautiful lady on the snow-white pony. She had long golden curls and a most dazzling smile, and Mr. Tickler thought he had never seen anything so lovely. But the snow-white pony was rather a disappointment. He was quite hard to manage and went through all his tricks so grudgingly that you thought he was going to lie down in the sawdust at any moment. The beautiful young lady spoke to him sweetly and gave him sugar, and the band began to play again very loudly, while they brought on a huge paper hoop. The young lady kissed her hand to the people and bowed and smiled, she sprang lightly on to the pony's back and tried to urge him on. But he simply wouldn't go. Again, the beautiful lady dismounted, and bowed and kissed her hand, but this time there were tears in her eyes and some rude boys in the sixpenny seats began to jeer. Mr. Tickler was overcome with grief, he couldn't bear to see the pretty lady made unhappy, so just as she tried to get the pony to jump for the third time, Mr. Tickler took out his handkerchief and gave one loud blow, and up sprang the pony and crashed clean through the centre of the hoop amid loud cheers from all the crowd.

The sudden shock must have brought the pony to his senses for he went through the rest of his performance without any nonsense, and when the lady bowed and kissed her hand for the last time, there were wild cheers and one young man threw a beautiful bunch of roses into the ring. As for Mr. Tickler he cheered more wildly than anyone, and he was so happy that he forgot all his troubles, forgetting even that his half hour was up long ago, and that Mrs. Tickler would be waiting on the steps of the van with a large stout broomhandle on her knee. Then came two clowns who fell into pails of water and splashed mops dripping with white-wash in each other's faces, and Mr. Tickler laughed so much that everybody in front turned round to look at him. Then came the Don Cossacks who threw knives at a target while they rode furiously round the ring. And Mr. Tickler shuddered fear-fully and sucked hard at the peppermint which had been given to him by an old lady in the next seat.

Last of all came the lions. There were only two of them and they did not roar very ferociously. But they looked very fierce and they lashed their tails against the bars of their cage, and opened their great mouths, so that when the trainer opened the door and went inside Mr. Tickler felt cold all down his back. He was so intensely excited that his nose began to itch, and before he could stop himself he had sneezed loudly and without thinking right in the middle of his magic handkerchief.

And then something really awful happened.

Mr. Tickler had sneezed right in the direction of

the lion's cage, and with one blow the bars had

caved in and out sprang the lions right into the ring and out among the people. Everybody screamed with terror, and made a mad rush for the way out. The lion tamer rushed after his lions and a big man in a top hat ran in and shouted out that there was no danger. But nobody stayed to listen to him. Everybody was rushing out of the Circus tent on to the green and down the village street as fast as their legs could carry them.

And Mr. Tickler ran with them. He ran without stopping all the way home to the van, without thinking once what he was going to say to Mrs. Tickler.

There she sat waiting for him, the broomhandle on her knee. But when she saw him come flying down the road as white as a sheet, even she thought something unusual must have happened.

" What is it ? " she said, as he came panting up.

" Lions got loose in the village," he said. " Quick. Horse the van."

Then Mrs. Tickler jumped up too, and they harnessed Dumpy and Nancy and rattled out of that village as though all the lions in the jungle were following them.

It was not until they had driven out about two miles that Mrs. Tickler remembered something.

" I suppose you lost that shilling in the excitement ? " she said, in the sort of tone which always boded something very unpleasant for Mr. Tickler.

But by some miracle he still had it in his coat pocket. And he was so thankful for his double escape that he handed it over to her without a word, and the extra threepence as well. But even then he didn't say anything about the magic handkerchief.

MR. TICKLER
TRIES THE MAGIC HANDKERCHIEF FOR THE SEVENTH TIME

NOW one of Mr. Tickler's jobs was to feed Mrs.
Tickler, and Mrs. Tickler had a very good appetite.

On moonlight nights Mr. Tickler might be seen,
wearing his coat with the big pockets, and
accompanied by Spark, the lurcher, wandering
off to the fields and woods. Later on Mr.
Tickler would return, his pockets rather bulgy,
and he would hand up to Mrs. Tickler a hare
or a brace of pheasants.

One evening Mr. Tickler had strolled off with Spark,

and on his return a fine fat hare was handed to Mrs. Tickler to be cooked for supper, which Mrs. Tickler always did on the stove inside her caravan.

It was such a very good supper that night that both Mr. and Mrs. Tickler over-slept themselves and the sun was rising as Policeman X was returning to his home eager for his breakfast, after a night in the woods in search of poachers.

Suddenly a most appetizing smell was wafted across Policeman X's nose.

" Ho ! " said the constable, " jugged hare, or I'm a marine."

Following the line of this enticing smell, he caught sight of the chimney of Mrs. Tickler's caravan.

Now Mr. and Mrs. Tickler had not eaten all the hare for supper, and what was left had remained in the little oven to keep hot for their breakfast; and it was the smell from this which had attracted the attention of Policeman X.

" Poachers without a doubt," he muttered, " and now to catch them red-handed."

But Mr. Tickler had just got up and as Policeman X came over the brow of the hill,

Mr. Tickler had seen his helmet. Snatching an almost nearly empty sardine tin—there was only one old sardine left in it—he at once pretended to be cooking it over a small fire he had just lit.

"A nice morning, sergeant," said Mr. Tickler chattily as the constable appeared beside him.

"Yes, and a nice smell of game," retorted the policeman.

"Game?" said Mr. Tickler innocently; "there's no game here. It must be my breakfast you can smell," pointing to the lonely sardine now simmering over the fire; "they do smell gamey when you get to the end of a tin and the oil has all run out. Smell it," said he, holding the ancient tin right under the constable's nose.

"Now, my lad, none of your games with me.

That's jugged hare I can smell, and it's here right under my nose;" and looking towards Mrs. Tickler's caravan, "I want to see inside that van," he said sternly.

Mr. Tickler was at his wits' end to know what to do, for he knew about the hare inside, and then suddenly he thought of his handkerchief. Snatching it up he gave such a vigorous nose blow that the policeman jumped six feet away, almost landing on the top of the fire Mr. Tickler had lit.

"You can't go in there; my wife is in her bath," said Mr. Tickler, once more blowing Policeman X ten yards out of the line of hare smell and farther away from the caravan.

"She always takes an hour over her bath," he said, which was not quite true, as Mrs. Tickler never had been known to have a morning bath.

The policeman sat down and waited a quarter of an hour, and then the thought of his own breakfast getting cold made him feel more and more

hungry.   Seeing that there was very little chance of his being able to get inside the caravan for some time, for the constable was a bashful man, he stumped off towards his own home, Mr. Tickler once more giving him just a gentle blow from his magic handkerchief to help him on his way.

MR. TICKLER
TRIES HIS HANDKERCHIEF FOR THE EIGHTH TIME

MR. TICKLER
TRIES HIS HANDKERCHIEF FOR THE EIGHTH TIME

Now Mr. Tickler, as you must have noticed, was a good-natured man. He did not mind working hard, looking after the animals and mending old pots and pans and rush chairs as they went through the villages, and collecting firewood and dodging policemen and things like that. He didn't even mind being grumbled at by Mrs. Tickler, which was quite as well, as nothing could have induced her to stop. And now he had got his magic handkerchief it made him happier than ever, especially as nobody else knew anything about it.

But there was one thing, or rather one person, who could always damp Mr. Tickler's spirits, and that was Mrs. Tickler's brother Joe. Joe was not, in fact, a very pleasant looking individual. He was tall and dark with a fierce squint in one eye. He

was supposed to have been a sailor, and certainly
he was tattooed all over with anchors and hearts
and girls' names as sailors generally are.   He did

not live with the Ticklers, but every now and then he would turn up from nowhere in particular and stay with them for a while. And whenever this happened it threw Mr. Tickler into the depths of gloom.

For Joe would do nothing but sit by the fire with Mrs. Tickler and say what a stupid man Mr. Tickler was, and Mrs. Tickler would agree with him. And Joe had a dreadful appetite, and he and his sister between them would fairly clear out the larder, only leaving the bones and fat ends for poor Mr. Tickler. Which, as Mr. Tickler found all the food and did all the work, was rather hard. Sometimes, it is true, Joe would go out and come back with a rabbit or a chicken for supper, but not very often. He generally said that his legs were giving him trouble.

Even the thought of the magic handkerchief did not cheer Mr. Tickler when he came home one night and found Joe sitting by the fire. "It is true that if I blew my nose on it," thought he, "I could send Joe flying over the other side of the fence, but what good would that do? He would only come back again and they would guess that there was something odd about the handkerchief, and they would just keep on worrying me until they found out." This dreadful thought made Mr. Tickler shiver, for he knew that if they did find out they would certainly take the handkerchief away from him. " No," he said to himself, " I shall have to find some other way of getting rid of Joe."

But poor Mr. Tickler was not a very clever man and he couldn't think of any other way. So Joe stayed on and sat by the fire saying what a poor fish Mr. Tickler was and eating up Mr. Tickler's dinner, while Mrs. Tickler scolded more than ever.

One day they sent Mr. Tickler out to pick blueberries. Not to make jam, for to tell the truth Mrs. Tickler was not fond of cooking, but to sell them in the small towns and the villages they passed through. Now picking blueberries, as I daresay you know, makes your back ache horribly, and the heather and the gorse they grow among prick your legs. That is why Joe and Mrs. Tickler did not go out to help him.

Mr. Tickler had picked and picked for nearly two hours, climbing up the hillside looking for the

largest and ripest berries. The sun came out and
shone on his back, making him very hot and tired,

so he went over to rest by a clump of bushes that bordered the narrow path running zig-zag up the hill. Presently he heard someone calling, and looking down he saw a boy running about and looking all round him as if he had lost someone. "Jock," called the boy and whistled, "Jock! Jock!" But no Jock answered.

Soon the boy came up level with Mr. Tickler. He was about twelve years old and he seemed very worried. His clothes were covered with straws and earth and leaves where he had been scrambling through thickets, and his coat sleeve was badly torn.

"Have you seen my pony?" he shouted, as soon as he came near Mr. Tickler.

"No," said Mr. Tickler. "There's been no ponies around here, and I've been here all the morning. What sort of pony is it?"

"He's a brown pony, with a white patch over one eye and his name is Jock," said the boy. "I missed him down there by Pike's Wood where I had to get off to take a message. And he doesn't know his way home, because he's only just come down here," added the boy sorrowfully.

75

Mr. Tickler was very upset. He could quite easily get upset about other people's troubles, which was one of the things about him that annoyed Joe and Mrs. Tickler.

"Well, well," he said to the boy. "Don't upset yourself. We'll find him for you. Me and my family are going all round here in the van, and if he's anywhere about you can bet we'll find him. Just tell me where you live and when I find him I'll bring him along."

The boy seemed to be comforted a little.

"That's awfully good of you," he said. "My name's Dick Grant and I live at Well House down there," and he pointed to the village lying in the valley.

"I know," said Mr. Tickler, "and I won't forget. Have some blueberries?" he added generously.

The boy took a handful and went on his way, whistling and calling for Jock.

Now would you believe it, when Mr. Tickler got back to his caravan at night, what should he see but a strange pony, feeding side by side with Dumpy and Nancy. And it was a brown pony with a white patch over one eye.

76

Mr. Tickler was just going to open his mouth and pour out the whole story when something in Joe's cross eye made him think better of it.

"After all," thought he, "they will certainly give me a reward when I take him back, and if I tell Joe, he will take it back himself and collar the money." So Mr. Tickler looked stupid, which was not very hard for him, and just said, "Hullo, a new horse? Where did he come from?"

"You shut your mouth," growled Joe.

"Got no more sense than a blessed baby," said Mrs. Tickler.

Then Mr. Tickler *was* glad that he had said nothing about the boy and his pony. For he began to think that perhaps the pony hadn't come all the way from Pike's Wood by himself.

That night, when Joe and Mrs. Tickler were asleep, Mr. Tickler got up and went softly out to the cart where Dumpy and the foal and the new pony were tethered. "Jock," he whispered, and patted his neck, and the pony rubbed his nose against him.

"It *is* Jock," said Mr. Tickler. "Now what can I do with him?"

For he knew somehow that Joe and Mrs. Tickler would not want to send him back. Dumpy was getting old and slow, and they had often said it was a pity that they couldn't get another horse. Or perhaps Joe wanted to sell Jock to some of those mysterious friends of his, who were always ready to buy anything from a watch and chain to a pony.

"If I try to ride him back now," said Mr. Tickler, "they'll be sure to hear me. And it's a long way to go."

All of a sudden he thought of his magic handkerchief.

He got up on Jock's back, patting him gently to keep him quiet, and then he gave just a little blow on the magic handkerchief. Just a little blow, not loud enough to awaken Joe or Mrs. Tickler, but enough to send Jock and Mr. Tickler fifty yards or so the other side of the hedge. Then he gave a louder blow, for he was out of earshot now, and he found himself half way down the road leading out of the wood into the village. And he blew and he blew, louder each time, until he found himself right outside the gates of Well House.

Enough to send them fifty yards over the hedge.

His nose was rather sore from all this blowing, but he was not going to give up now. He jumped off Jock's back and aimed one mighty blow at the pony, which sent him flying over the gates of Well House drive into safety and nearly knocked Mr. Tickler backwards into the ditch.

And when Colonel Grant came out the next morning and found Jock grazing quietly in his own grounds he couldn't think how he had got there. But Dick had an idea that the queer tramp-looking man had had something to do with it.

Joe and Mrs. Tickler were equally at a loss to think how Jock could have got away, but they had no idea that Mr. Tickler had anything to do with it. They thought he was far too stupid.

And Mr. Tickler went quite happily about his work, although Joe and Mrs. Tickler were crosser than usual, and although he knew that he had given up a reward of, well, ten shillings at least, or perhaps even a pound.

But you will, I am sure, be glad to know that he did get something out of it after all, for Joe was so disgusted at losing the pony, which he had meant to sell to one of his friends, that he went away very soon afterwards and he never came back to stay with the Ticklers again.

MR. TICKLER
TRIES HIS HANDKERCHIEF
FOR THE NINTH AND LAST TIME

MR. TICKLER
TRIES HIS HANDKERCHIEF FOR THE
NINTH AND LAST TIME

" THERE'S no end to what this handkerchief of mine can do," said Mr. Tickler one day soon after Joe had gone away. "I must have a great big blow one day and see what it really can accomplish."

Little did Mr. Tickler think when he said this of the awful result that this last big blow would have.

Sometime afterwards he was sitting on an up-turned bucket thinking of the marvels of his magic handkerchief. He was again wondering what would happen if he gave his really biggest blow, and hardly had the thought come into his inquisitive head when he decided to try it.

The caravan and donkey-cart were all ready to start, and it took Mr. Tickler some few minutes to work up steam for this last great effort. Many and many were the deep breaths he took, and his face and nose got more and more red as he prepared for it; but at last it came with one enormous explosion, and the result was even worse than you or I could have expected, for Mr. Tickler saw Mrs. Tickler and her caravan, Nancy, Dumpy and his cart, Spark and the Cock-a-doodles suddenly hurled up into the sky. It was a terrible sight for poor Mr. Tickler, and as he watched all his world fly higher and higher into the clouds, he sat down on his bucket and wept.

For some time he sat disconsolately gazing into the sky, salt tears running down his cheeks and dripping from the ends of his beard.

In the middle of his weeping a sudden swishing through the air as of something rapidly falling made him look up, and he saw just above his head Mrs. Tickler's tea-kettle parachuting down, fixed on the handle of his blue umbrella.

As these dropped to earth with a loud " plop " at his feet, he waited, hoping against hope that other things would follow; but after some time he rose to collect all that was left to him of his home —his wife's tea-kettle and his own umbrella. As he did this he noticed the big red handkerchief lying on the ground at his feet. On seeing this,

Mr. Tickler saw them suddenly hurled into the air.

Mrs. Tickler's kettle parachuting down.

Mr. Tickler flew into a violent rage, and jumped and stamped on what he considered was the cause of all his trouble. And then a most extraordinary thing happened, which neither you nor I could have imagined, for the magic handkerchief suddenly rose in the air, carrying Mr. Tickler, the umbrella and tea-kettle with it.

Up and up and up, higher it rose, and more

and more giddy Mr. Tickler felt whenever he

looked over the edge, until at last he saw a small cloud far, far away above him. Now I don't suppose you will ever guess what Mr. Tickler found when he reached that cloud, but, believe me, or believe me not, in the centre of it was Mrs. Tickler, looking more beautiful than he had ever seen her before. Bump went the magic handkerchief against the side of the cloud, and on to it jumped Mr. Tickler; which ends this story, as it should do, because, for we all know, they both lived happily ever afterwards with the tea-kettle, the blue umbrella, and the magic handkerchief.